For my CA and EMLA critique partners
—M.W.L.

To Hayes and Pippa
—B.H.F.

THIS IS A BORZOI BOOK PUBLISHED BY ALFRED A. KNOPF

Text copyright © 2018 by Megan Wagner Lloyd

Jacket art and interior illustrations copyright © 2018 by Brianne Farley

All rights reserved. Published in the United States by Alfred A. Knopf,

an imprint of Random House Children's Books, a division of Penguin Random House LLC, New York.

Knopf, Borzoi Books, and the colophon are registered trademarks of Penguin Random House LLC.

Visit us on the Web! rhcbooks.com

Educators and librarians, for a variety of teaching tools,

visit us at RHTeachersLibrarians.com

Library of Congress Cataloging-in-Publication Data is available upon request.

ISBN 978-1-5247-7367-0 (trade) — ISBN 978-1-5247-7368-7 (lib. bdg.) —

ISBN 978-1-5247-7369-4 (ebook)

The text of this book is set in 12-point American Typewriter.

The illustrations were created using ink and gouache, and finished digitally.

MANUFACTURED IN CHINA

October 2018

10 9 8 7 6 5 4 3 2 1

First Edition

Building Books

Megan Wagner Lloyd

Illustrated by Brianne Farley

Alfred A. Knopf
New York

Katie loved building with blocks.

She loved the way they clicked as she pressed them together.

She loved the way they wobbled as she stacked them up high.

She even loved the way they crashed as they toppled to the floor.

But most of all, Katie loved the way she felt when she built something brand-new.

Owen loved reading books.

He loved the way they swooshed as he pulled them off the shelves.

He loved the way they rustled as he turned the pages.

He even loved the way the paper smelled.
But most of all, Owen loved the way he felt
when he read something brand-new.

Katie had to read books for school.

But Katie did not want to read.

When Katie tried to read, her hands felt squirmy.

When Katie tried to read, her legs felt wiggly.

When Katie tried to read, she wished she were building instead.

So, when she was supposed to be reading . . .
Katie built castles.
She built cities.
She built worlds.

"Building's the best!" proclaimed Katie.

"Nope. Reading rules," countered Owen.

Katie scowled at her brother.

He glared right back.

They scowled and glared—
and they each wondered what was wrong
with the other one.

"Building's better!"

"Reading is!"

The librarian seemed to appear out of nowhere.

"May I suggest a suitable alternative?"

"A stack of books for you,"
the librarian said to Katie.
"To read."

"And a stack for you,"
she said to Owen. "To shelve."

Katie squirmed and wiggled in the big library chair.

She missed the clicking and the wobbling and the crashing of her blocks.

But most of all, she missed building something brand-new.

Katie stood up. "Building's *way* better than reading," she said.

But Owen didn't answer.
His nose was buried in a book.

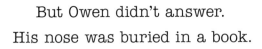

Katie picked a thick book from the
library shelves.

She wanted to see if it could
balance on its side.

It could.

Katie picked out more books.

She liked the way they swooshed as she pulled them off
the shelves.

Katie began to build.

She almost finished building a castle, but when she
reached up to balance the last book on the very tippy-top—

Katie looked around to make sure no one was watching . . .

And then she began to read.

Katie's hands stopped feeling squirmy.

Her legs stopped feeling wiggly.

She liked the way the pages rustled as she turned them.

She even liked the way the paper smelled.

But most of all, Katie liked reading something brand-new.

She read another book. And another.

And another.

Katie visited castles.

She explored cities.

She discovered worlds.

Owen finished his book with a snap and
looked about in surprise.

He had never seen so many books on the
floor before.

He hoped the librarian wouldn't make him
shelve them all.

He liked reading books, not arranging them.
But . . .

One book was balanced on its side.

Owen found himself wondering if another book could balance on top of it.

It could.

Owen looked around to make sure no one was watching . . .

And then he began to build.

He liked the way the books thunked as he pressed them together.

He liked the way they wobbled as he stacked them up high.

He even liked the way they crashed as they toppled to the floor.

But most of all, he liked building something brand-new.

"Look what I made!" Owen called to Katie.

At the same time, Katie ran to Owen.

"Have you read this?" she squealed. "What about this one? And this one? And this one?" Katie hugged an armful of books. "I love reading!!!!!!!"

Owen grinned. "And I love building!"

Katie and Owen sat down in the big library chair
and read, together.

And then they began to build.